# MEET ALL THESE FRIENDS IN BUZZ BOOKS:

Thomas the Tank Engine
Fireman Sam
The Animals of Farthing Wood
James Bond Junior
Joshua Jones
Rupert
Babar

First published in Great Britain in 1994
by Buzz Books
an imprint of Reed Children's Books
Michelin House, 81 Fulham Road, London SW3 6RB
and Auckland, Melbourne, Singapore and Toronto

ISBN 1 85591 371 2

Printed in Italy by Olivotto

# THE MASKED
# MOTORCYCLIST

Story by Norman Redfern
Illustrations by Arkadia

Charley was working hard at the Last Chance Garage. She was building a new radio to pick up distress signals from all over the city. The Biker Mice were busy, too – mopping the garage floor!

"Aw, Charley," moaned Modo. "Do we really have to do this?"

"You're the ones that spilled the oil!" said Charley.

She tried tuning the radio again. Suddenly, the speaker crackled.

"Emergency! Fires and explosions at 15th and J Street!"

Throttle, Vinnie and Modo raced to their bikes.

"Oh no you don't!" cried Charley. "This time, I'm getting in on the action. I've got –"

Throttle didn't let her finish.

"Sorry, Charley," he said. "But this is a job for *men*. C'mon, bro's, let's rock –"

"– and ride!" cried Modo and Vinnie, as they sped out of the garage.

Charley watched them ride away. She wasn't pleased.

The Biker Mice raced to the scene. They passed fire engines, cut off from the blaze by deep craters in the road. Throttle had a good idea who was to blame.

"Limburger!" he shouted, as they jumped their bikes over the craters.

Then, as they came nearer to the fire, Vinnie heard something. From inside a block of flats came a desperate cry for help.

"Someone's trapped," he said. "C'mon!"

The Biker Mice smashed in through the doors of the burning building. Inside, the frightened shouts were louder than before, but there was no one in sight. Then Modo spotted something. The voice was coming from a tape recorder on the lobby floor!

"Ain't no one trapped here," he said angrily.

"I can fix dat, Mouses!" snarled Greasepit.

Limburger's henchman was standing in the
doorway, with a foam cannon aimed straight
at the Biker Mice. With one squeeze of the
trigger, Greasepit filled the lobby with fast-
setting foam.

"Can't move," said Vinnie.

"Might as well stick around," agreed Modo.

Greasepit laughed horribly. The Mice were
trapped and the fire was spreading into the
lobby. Then they heard the roar of an engine.

Suddenly something crashed into Greasepit,
sending him skidding across the floor and out
through the far wall. In his place in the
doorway stood a gleaming motorcycle.

Its rider's face was hidden behind a dark visor, but there was something the Masked Motorcyclist couldn't hide. She was a woman.

The mysterious biker hit a button, and diamond-lasers popped out of the wheel-hubs. They cut through the foam and in moments the Biker Mice were free.

"Thanks, ma'am," said Throttle. "Great work!"

"Great bike!" said Modo.

"Great outfit!" added Vinnie.

They used Greasepit's foam cannon to fill the craters in the road. As the foam set, the fire engines raced across to tackle the blaze.

Charley had just finished mopping the floor when the Biker Mice returned to the garage. They skidded across the clean floor, leaving muddy tyre tracks.

"So, did you manage to save the city again?" asked Charley.

"Not only did we manage to save the city," began Modo.

"But we met the single most awesome biker babe in the entire universe!" said Vinnie.

Charley picked up the mop and wiped away the fresh mud.

"Whoopee," she said, scornfully.

Across the city, Lawrence Limburger had another mission for Greasepit.

"Plutark needs crude oil," he told him, "and plenty of it. I must locate a supply."

"Uh…like an oilfield, Boss?" asked Greasepit.

Limburger was deep in thought.

"I've got it!" he said at last. "An oilfield! Get Karbunkle to bring in Cody. His Rustmobile will melt oil pipes like a blowtorch on butter!"

That night, at the garage, the Mice tuned
Charley's new radio to their favourite rock
station. Suddenly, a terrified scream broke
through the music.

"A distress call!" cried Charley. "It's coming
from the oilfield. Let's go!"

"No dice," said Vinnie. "This is he-man work, remember?"

"It's for your own good," said Throttle. "You might get hurt."

Charley was furious. She turned on her heels and stomped upstairs to her bedroom.

The Biker Mice raced to the oilfield. Greasepit was driving the Oil-Guzzler, and Corroder Cody was in his Rustmobile. He sprayed the oil pipes with gas which melted the metal in seconds. As the oil poured out, Greasepit sucked it up into the Guzzler's tanks.

"Quick, bro's!" said Throttle. "Cody's almost at the main derrick!"

They sped after the Rustmobile. Greasepit tried to stop them. Throttle spotted a stack of oil drums.

"Let's give Greasepit a whole barrel of laughs!" he shouted.

Vinnie used a flare to cut the chain holding the oil drums. The barrels tumbled down into the Guzzler's path.

"Take dis, Mouses!" said Greasepit

He fired the Guzzler's cannons at the Biker Mice. Vinnie swerved, but there was another biker heading towards him. It was the Masked Motorcyclist!

Vinnie pulled away, but it was too late. The mystery biker bounced off him, out of control.

Greasepit put his foot down and aimed the Guzzler at the gap between the oil drums. But the oil drums had been stacked against a tank full of explosive gas!

The Guzzler smashed into the gas tank. There was a massive explosion, and the Guzzler was blown sky-high.

Corroder Cody had reached the main derrick.

"Time to blow yer stack, big fella," he chuckled, blasting out another cloud of gas.

Then he looked up. The Guzzler was falling
fast towards the Rustmobile. But as it crashed
down, the evil gas swirled around and melted
the Guzzler!

"Bro's! Look!" cried Vinnie.

The Masked Motorcyclist was lying on the ground, her bike by her side. She wasn't moving.

The Biker Mice carried her back to the Last Chance Garage. Vinnie ran up to Charley's room. She was fast asleep.

"Charley! Wake up!" he shouted. "The Masked Motorcyclist's hurt. We can't get her helmet off. Help us – please!"

He shook the bed – and the sleeping figure's head rolled off. It was a dummy!

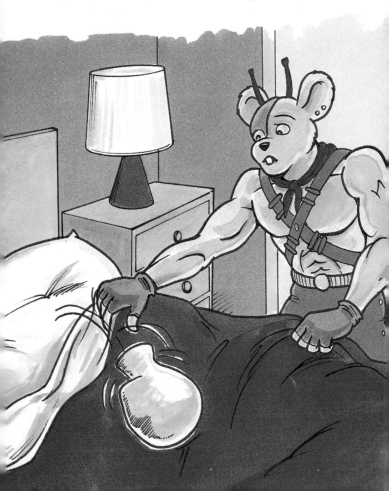

Downstairs in the garage, Throttle and Modo
gently slipped off the Masked Motorcyclist's
helmet. She opened her eyes and…

"Hi, guys! Surprise!"

It was Charley.

"You could have told us," said Throttle.

"I tried," said Charley, "but you never listen. I was testing out a new bike for the Army."

"But Charley," said Modo, "the reason we didn't want you with us was 'cause you might get hurt – and you did!"

"I know," said Charley. "But I didn't get

hurt because I'm a *woman*. I got hurt because
I did something dangerous."

She rubbed her head and grinned at
Throttle, Modo and Vinnie.

"And now, the Masked Motorcyclist could
use a root beer – if you he-men can find the
refrigerator!"